MW00979015

To all of the little kids with crazy ideas and big dreams,
take charge and never give up.

And

To Louie and Mikey, may you be inspired to do things
you never thought possible, just as you've done for me.

www.mascotbooks.com

She's the Boss

For more information, please contact:
Mascot Kids, an imprint of Amplify Publishing Group
620 Herndon Parkway, Suite 320
Herndon, VA 20170
info@mascotbooks.com

Library of Congress Control Number: 2022912871

CPSIA Code: PRKF1122A

ISBN-13: 978-1-63755-278-0

Printed in China

ALANA TOULOPOULOS
ILLUSTRATED BY LARA CALLEJA

Hi! My name is Briony.
Are you ready to take this journey with me?

I have a story to tell,
and I'd like you to help me do it well!

One, two, three.
Are you ready to snap with me?

Because . . .

Oooo, oooo! *I have important work to do!*

SNAP, SNAP

2022
GLUE

At my desk is where I work,
creating all of my new
artwork.

Now, say it with me . . .
One, two, three.

*Oooo, oooo! I have
important work to do!*

SNAP, SNAP.

Today, I'll shave some pencils and have them decorated.
The kids at school will be elated.

Pick, stick.

Shave, wave.

Twist, glitz.

AND . . . VOILA!

Come to school with me.

I'm going to make so much money, just wait and see!

I will sell my pencils to everyone,

then use the earnings to buy something fun!

What's that? Do you see the people over there?
It seems like they're looking for new clothes to wear.

They're heading to a shelter. Do you see that, too?
It looks like some people need more than I do.

I have an idea! Now, when I sell my new creations,
the proceeds will go to local foundations.

Let's go do some good! Don't you think we should?

Oooo, oooo! I have important work to do!

SNAP, SNAP.

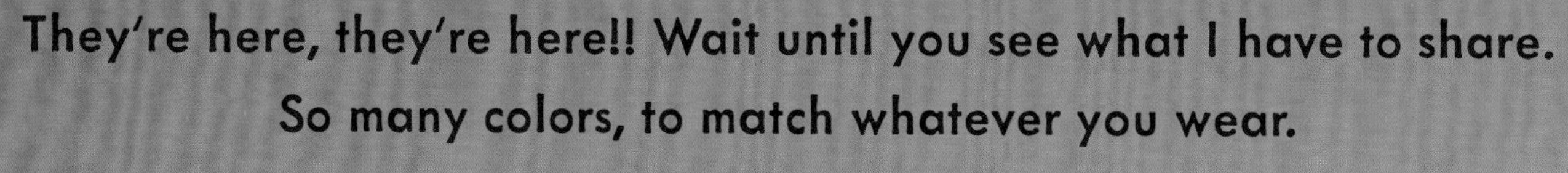

They're here, they're here!! Wait until you see what I have to share.
So many colors, to match whatever you wear.

Each one has their own design.
They are simply divine.

Take your pick,
green or blue.
Some even have
glitter glue!

There is also
black and white.
Surely, you'll find
one that's just
right.

Thank you for waiting in line.
Would you like to purchase my new design?

I will be donating to those in need.
The homeless and hungry are who I plan to feed.

Watch me go! I'm earning money, see?

Come on and say it with me . . .

Oooo, oooo! I have important work to do!

SNAP, SNAP.

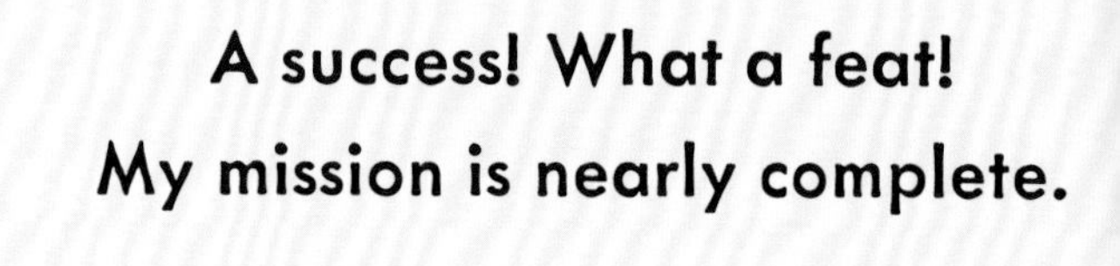

A success! What a feat!
My mission is nearly complete.

But, before the day is done,
let's say it again, because it's so much fun!

Oooo, oooo! I have important work to do!

SNAP, SNAP.

AB || CD

Now, let's go give this donation
to the Homeless Foundation.
I can't wait to bring this money there,
It will help buy people food to eat and clothes to wear.

Hopefully, they will find
that what we did was really kind.

My work here is done.
It was a busy day, but lots of fun!

Come with me, it's time to head back.
Tonight, I can make another pack.

I know what to say now, do you?

Oooo, oooo! I have important work to do!

SNAP, SNAP.

Oh, I must say,
this was the best day!
Now it's time to rest,
so tomorrow I can be my best.

2022

HOMELESS FOUNDATION

Thanks for coming with me, friend!
My story is over, but it's not the end.

I can tell you one thing for sure:
I LOVE BEING AN ENTREPRENEUR.

Wait until you see what's next. I'll give you a clue . . .

Oooo, oooo! I have important work to do!

SNAP, SNAP.

ABOUT THE AUTHOR

Alana Toulopoulos lives north of Boston with her husband and their two children. She graduated from Bentley University and then went on to business school. Alana has spent much of her career focused on health and wellness initiatives. She currently works in the digital health space. Her favorite role, however, is that of a mother to her two most precious gifts, Louie and Mikey.

This is Alana's first children's book, which was inspired by her love for children and her hope that they all have equal opportunities to succeed, both personally and professionally.

ABOUT THE ILLUSTRATOR

Lara is a Filipino children's book illustrator. She finished a degree in computer science but now works full time as an illustrator. Drawing has always been her passion. She loves to work digitally and traditionally with watercolors and gouache. Lara has worked on many children's books from around the world.

ACKNOWLEDGMENTS

Overwhelming gratitude to M.A.T, the original pencil shaver and love of my life.

And

To Mom, Dad, Jeremy, and Elisia, for the type of childhood that inspires me every day.